GW00725644

Earl

the EMU™

* God has a purpose for those who are different.

by Pat Winston

Illustrated by Cathy Allen

Copyright © 2000 by Patricia Trice Winston.

All rights reserved. Written permission must be secured from the author to use or reproduce any
part of this book, except for brief quotations in critical reviews or articles.
"EARL the EMU™" and the emu design are trademarks of Patricia Trice Winston.

EARL the EMU™

Published by:
Light Way Publications
P.O. Box 10123
Jackson, TN 38308-0102
Phone: (901) 660-5057
Toll Free: (888) 815-0445
E-mail: earlemu@aol.com

www.earlemu.com

Produced by:
Renee´ Smith, The Write Connection

67 Channing Way Jackson, TN 38305

Cover Design/Media Design Group, Jackson TN

Printed and Color Separations done by Amica International Inc.,

ISBN: 0-9702821-0-9
Library of Congress Catalog Number 00-191610

First edition, 2000
10 9 8 7 6 5 4 3 2 1

Printed in Korea

To my family and special friends.

I thank God for you and your loving support and encouragement.

NOTE: Emu birds are not pets. Children should **<u>never</u>** go close to them or try to pet them unless they are accompanied by an adult.

A portion of the proceeds from the sale of this book goes to the
Excellent Achievers Require Love (EARL) Foundation
for the empowerment of inner-city youth and homeless women and children.

For more information about the EARL Foundation, please call or write:

The EARL Foundation
P. O. Box 10123
Jackson, TN 38308-0102
Phone: (901) 660-5057
Toll Free: (888) 815-0445
E-mail: earlemu@aol.com
www.earlemu.com

"Commit thy works unto the Lord, and thy thoughts shall be established."

—Proverbs 16:3 kjv

Farmer and Mrs. Berry lived on a farm in the little town of Sunnyville. Farmer Berry always wore purple overalls and Mrs. Berry was always in the kitchen fixing something good to eat. They were very happy, because their grandson, Jason, was coming from the city to visit them.

Jason enjoyed visiting his grandparents. He liked playing with the farm animals. There were many animals on the Berry Farm. There were cows, pigs, ducks, and chickens. Jason's favorite farm friends were Duke the Dog, Roscoe the Rooster, Hattie the Hen, and Max the Baby Chick.

Jason was different from other children. He could understand what the farm animals said to each other. He was the only one who could. Jason liked all the farm animals, and all the farm animals liked Jason. They were good friends.

Jason was different from other children in another way, also. Something was wrong with one of his legs, so he wore a leg brace. Jason couldn't run as fast as other boys and girls. He had a hard time keeping up when they played games like Hide 'n' Seek and Kick Ball.

Jason's grandparents always told him that all God's creatures are special. People who are different play an important part in the lives of others. God has a purpose for those who are different.

Farmer Berry had been planning a big surprise for Jason's visit. Farmer Berry didn't tell Mrs. Berry, Jason, or the other farm animals what it was. It would be the biggest surprise they had ever seen!

The first morning of Jason's visit, Farmer Berry rose very early. This was the big day!

"What's the big surprise?" asked Mrs. Berry as Farmer Berry was getting in his truck.

"It'll be here soon," replied Farmer Berry. "You're going to like it."

Mrs. Berry and Jason waved good-bye as Farmer Berry drove away.

Later that evening Farmer Berry came back to the Berry Farm. When he drove up, a trailer was hitched to the back of the truck. Something was sticking out of the trailer and bobbing up and down. Whatever it was, it certainly looked funny.

"He's here. He's here!" shouted Jason as he went to meet Farmer Berry. All the farm animals followed Jason to see the big surprise.

"Hi, Grandpops," smiled Jason when he reached the truck. "What's in the trailer?" he asked.

"Yes, what's in the trailer?" said Mrs. Berry as she walked up the driveway.

"I wonder what it is?" crowed Roscoe the Rooster.

"What's all the fuss about?" chirped Max the Baby Chick.

"Bi-i-i-g deal!" clucked Hattie the Hen.

"Well, everybody, this is the surprise!" smiled Farmer Berry as he led the funny-looking bird out of the trailer. "This is Earl, and Earl is an emu. Earl has come to live with us on the farm."

"It's a what?" asked Max.

"Some kind of mule," crowed Roscoe.

"Looks more like a bird to me," barked Duke.

"Some kind of bird, indeed. Hmff!" clucked Hattie the Hen. "Look at that long, skinny neck and those great, big eyes on that little, bitty head. That's not a bird, it's a garden hose with wings!"

"Oh, Hattie," said Duke.

"Well, it is! It's not as good-looking as hens and roosters are," clucked Hattie.

Little Max didn't know what all the fuss was about. He liked the funny-looking bird. He thought Earl was a nice name, and he hoped they could be friends.

"Wow, Grandpops! Can this bird fly?" asked Jason.

"No-o-o," answered Farmer Berry. "Earl is a fast-running bird. God made this bird different from other birds."

"This bird is different, just like I am. God has a purpose for those who are different, right Granny?" asked Jason.

"That's right, Jason," said Mrs. Berry.

"Remember, everything God makes is special," said Farmer Berry.

"Welcome, Earl," said Mrs. Berry as she patted the emu's wings. "We're very glad you're here."

"Well, I'm not glad you're here," clucked Hattie the Hen.

"Me, either," added Roscoe the Rooster. "Who wants to play with a funny-looking bird like that?"

Earl's feelings were hurt when the other farm animals made fun of him. Earl was sad, because he really wanted to be their friend.

"Don't worry, Earl," said Jason as he patted the emu bird. "Sometimes people make fun of me, too. All of God's creatures are special, and God loves us all just the way we are."

Then Jason turned to the farm animals and said, "Come, on. Let's go play."

All of them except Earl followed Jason. Duke the Dog, Hattie the Hen, Roscoe the Rooster, and Max the Baby Chick went with Jason, but Earl wasn't sure if he should go.

"Come on, Earl!" shouted Jason. "Come play with us!"

Earl ran to catch up with them, but
the emu bird wasn't used to being on a farm.
First he tripped over some clumps of grass . . .

. . . and bumped his head on a low tree limb.

Then he stumbled on a rock . . .

. . . and got tangled up in a bush.

"Hey, look at Mr. Clumsy!" said Hattie.

"Ha, ha!" laughed Roscoe. "Earl's so clumsy that he trips over his own feet."

"Clumsy, clumsy, what a bum-sy," clucked Hattie.

"Hey, stop that!" said Jason. "Don't ever make fun of others. All of God's creatures are special, and God loves us all just the way we are."

Hattie and Roscoe weren't too sure about Earl being special. They stopped calling Earl names, but they still laughed when Earl stumbled.

"Look, here's the creek. I'm going to play with my sailboat," said Jason. He waved to Mrs. Berry, who smiled as she watched from a short distance.

Jason sailed his toy boat in the creek, Duke chased colorful butterflies, and the others went swimming. Soon they were all having fun.

Suddenly, Little Max went too far out into the creek. "Come back toward the grass," said Hattie the Hen.

"Yes, come back," crowed Roscoe the Rooster, "or else the water will pull you away."

Little Max tried to swim back toward the creek bank, but it was too late. The water was pulling him away.

"Help! Help!" cried Little Max. "I can't make it back!"

Jason knew that Little Max was in trouble. He looked around for a way to help, but Max was way out in the water.

"Do something, Roscoe!" squawked Hattie.

"I can't reach him. He's too far away!" yelled Roscoe.

"I can't reach him, either," barked Duke.

"Help me! Help me!" cried Little Max. "Somebody, please save me!"

"I'm close enough, Little Max!" yelled Earl. "My neck is very long. When I stretch out my neck, you grab hold of it!"

Max the Baby Chick was moving further and further away. Earl the Emu quickly stretched out his long neck.

Little Max tried to grab Earl's neck, but a big wave knocked the baby chick further out.

"Oh, no!" squawked Hattie. "Little Max will never make it."

"Try again! Try again!" yelled Jason. "You can do it, Earl!"

Earl knew he had to hurry. He took a deep breath and stretched out as far as he could. Earl stretched out so far that his head went under the water!

"It worked! It worked! Look, Hattie. Little Max was able to grab Earl's neck!" crowed Roscoe.

Little Max grabbed Earl's neck just in time. The baby chick was able to walk safely along Earl's neck until he was back on the grass of the creek bank.

"Wow, Granny, did you and Grandpops see what Earl just did?" asked Jason as Farmer Berry and Mrs. Berry arrived.

"Yes, we did," answered Mrs. Berry.

"We heard a lot of yelling, so we came as fast as we could," added Farmer Berry.

"Earl just saved Little Max!" said Jason as he pointed toward the emu.

"You certainly did, Earl," said Roscoe the Rooster. "That long neck of yours is really something!"

"Earl's a hero!" barked Duke the Dog.

"Thank you for saving Little Max," said Hattie the Hen. "I'm sorry we made fun of you and your long neck."

"You're welcome," said Earl happily.

"If it hadn't been for Earl's long neck, Little Max never would have made it," said Jason. "Gee, Grandpops. Now I know what you and Granny mean. God really does have a purpose for those who are different. Just like Earl."

"Just like you, too, Jason," replied Farmer Berry. "If it weren't for you, Earl wouldn't have been at the creek to save Max. You're the one who made Earl feel welcome and asked him to come along."

"All of us are special, Jason," said Mrs. Berry. "God doesn't ever want us to make fun of others just because they're different than we are."

"Well, I'm never going to make fun of others again," clucked Hattie.

"Me, either," agreed Roscoe.

"God has a light that shines in all of us," smiled Farmer Berry. "When God makes some people and animals different, that light shines especially bright inside them. It reminds us that God has a purpose for those who are different."

"Yes," agreed Mrs. Berry. "All of God's creatures are special, and God loves all of us exactly like we are."

Jason smiled happily as Farmer and Mrs. Berry returned to the house. He was glad he had come to visit his grandparents.

"Come on," said Jason to the farm animals. "I'll pull you around the farm in the red wagon."

"I can pull them in the red wagon, too," said Earl the Emu. "We can take turns pulling our friends around the farm."

Duke the Dog, Hattie the Hen, Roscoe the Rooster, and Max the Baby Chick all hopped in the red wagon. Then Jason and Earl took turns pulling them around the Berry Farm the rest of the afternoon. They knew they would all be friends for a long, long time.

THE END

SPECIAL MESSAGE FROM EARL:

Boys and girls, you're special exactly like you are. God loves you and Earl does, too!